By R.P. Huttinga

The Adventures Of
Aussie and Otis

Welcome Home

◆ FriesenPress

Suite 300 - 990 Fort St
Victoria, BC, V8V 3K2
Canada

www.friesenpress.com

ISBN
978-1-5255-1994-9 (Hardcover)
978-1-5255-1995-6 (Paperback)
978-1-5255-1996-3 (eBook)

1. JUVENILE FICTION, ANIMALS, DOGS

Distributed to the trade by The Ingram Book Company

In loving memory of Aussie
2000 - 2017

The morning sun was about to shine on Aussie's bed. It was her favorite time of the day. After many years of running races as a sled dog, Aussie liked to feel the warmth of the sun on her old body. Something about today was going to be different, but what was it, she thought. Then, suddenly, Mrs. B came down the stairs and they said together, at the same time,

"THE PUPPY IS COMING TODAY!"

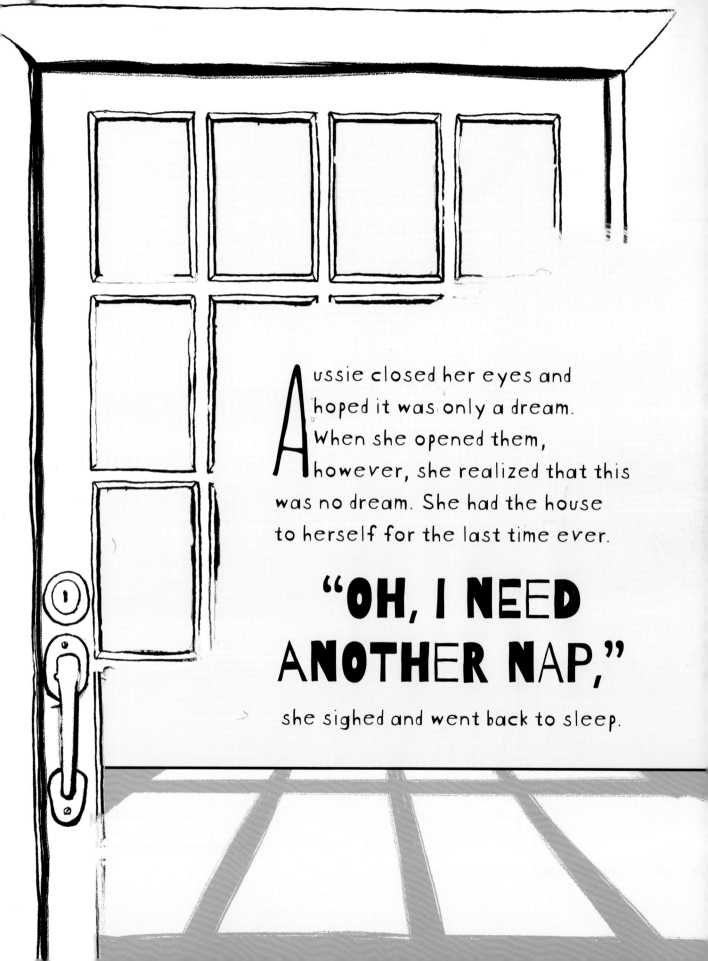

Aussie closed her eyes and hoped it was only a dream. When she opened them, however, she realized that this was no dream. She had the house to herself for the last time ever.

"OH, I NEED ANOTHER NAP,"

she sighed and went back to sleep.

Aussie suddenly awoke as the front door opened and a little puppy peeked inside his new home. He started sniffing with his little nose all the new smells. He found his way to the kitchen, walked up to Aussie on her bed, looked at her and said, "You have a large nose!"

Aussie smiled and replied, "You must be Otis.

WELCOME TO MY HOME.

I'm Aussie."

"Your bed looks soft. May I sit beside you?" Otis asked.

"Yes, I will move over and give you some room," Aussie replied.

"You know, Aussie, I am a pug puppy who likes to play games. Do you like to play games?" Otis asked.

"Well," she told him, "when I was younger my friends and I would play in the snow."

Otis had a funny look on his little face and asked, "Um, Aussie? What's snow?"

"It's white and fluffy and fun to play in," Aussie answered.

"I like to play hide-and-go-seek," said Otis. "Have you ever played that before?"

"**N**o, how do you play that game?" asked Aussie.

"You close your eyes and count to 50, and I will hide. Then you come and try and find me. Now close your eyes, and no peeking!" Otis explained. Aussie closed her eyes and started to count, "One, two, three..." Otis called out,

"SLOWER, PLEASE!"

Then he noticed the big chair by the window and thought, **THIS LOOKS LIKE A GREAT PLACE TO HIDE!** Aussie continued counting,

"37, 38, 39..."

then slowly fell asleep.

Otis looked under the chair. No Aussie yet! **MAYBE THIS ISN'T A GOOD SPOT,** he thought. Otis quietly moved from behind the chair, trying not to make any noise, when he heard snoring. "Hey, wait a minute!" Otis said as he came out from behind the couch. He walked into the kitchen and saw Aussie sleeping on her bed. Otis cleared his throat. Aussie opened one eye and grinned.

"Aussie, how old are you?" Otis asked curiously.

"I'm 14 years old," she answered.

"Wow, I'm eight weeks old. Are we close?" asked Otis.

"No Otis, we are many years apart," laughed Aussie.

"Aussie, what did you do when you were younger?" Otis continued.

"Here, I'll move over a bit on the bed and tell you about my amazing life," Aussie answered as Otis snuggled in.

"When I was younger, I became a sled dog. My friends and I would pull the sleigh through the mountains, and across a frozen lake, covered in snow."

"What was the biggest race you ran?" asked Otis.

"It was the Yukon Quest. It was a thousand miles, and it took my team 14 days to finish. We came in 11th place!"

Otis' eyes were getting heavy. As he was falling asleep he thought,

I WOULD LIKE TO BE A SLED DOG SOMEDAY.

The next morning, Mrs. B put the dogs into the van and headed off to the park. As they approached it, Otis noticed the large fir trees. "Wow, they're so tall!" he exclaimed. Mrs. B walked along ahead of them down the trail. Otis stopped to listen, and asked,

"AUSSIE, WHAT'S THAT SOUND?"

"It's a stream. I go down every day to get a drink. You can join me!"

As they headed towards the stream, they met another dog who introduced herself. Aussie told Otis her name was Aspen.

"Good morning Aussie!" she said. "Who's this little fellow?"

"I'M OTIS, AND I AM A PUG!"

"Nice to meet you, little one. Have a great day Aussie," said Aspen.

"You too, Aspen," Aussie replied.

As they approached the stream, Aussie told him to follow
her. The rocks were slippery and wet. Otis slowly
and carefully trailed Aussie. When they reached the
rushing water Aussie lowered her head and started to
drink. Otis watched and then did the same.

Then suddenly, Otis stopped drinking as he
noticed both of their reflections in the water.
Then he looked at Aussie and asked,

"COULD YOU TEACH ME
TO BECOME A

SLED DOG?"

Aussie stopped drinking and looked at her little friend. "You
know, sled dogs are big and strong," she told him.

"I'll do every thing you teach me!" Otis promised.

Aussie smiled.

"I was a puppy once. The first thing you must learn is to walk beside me and keep your head up. Watch me, then it's your turn."

EASY, Otis thought, until...

"WATCH OUT FOR THAT BRANCH!"

Aussie warned Otis, but it was too late. Otis tripped and fell into the mud.

"Oh no!" Mrs. B said when she saw Otis. "Looks like you're going to get your first bath!"

"What's a bath?" Otis wondered out loud.

Aussie grinned and said, "You're going to love it!"

When they got home, Mrs. B went downstairs to fill the laundry tub with water, then called out, "Otis! Time for your bath!" She came back and then carried him downstairs and lowered Otis into the tub.. He tried his best to catch the bubbles while she cleaned him.

With Otis all clean,
Mrs. B wrapped him up in a big fluffy towel.

After supper, Otis snuggled in beside Aussie. As he was about to fall asleep, he grinned and thought,

MY FIRST DAY AS A SLED DOG WAS AMAZING!

I CAN'T WAIT FOR OUR NEXT ADVENTURE.

THE END

SPECIAL THANKS to Penny Stone at the Victoria Humane Society who has placed over 300 sled dogs into forever homes.

A portion of sales will be donated to Victoria Humane Society in loving memory of Aussie.

Dog rescue organizations

1. Victoria Humane Society www.victoriahumanesociety.com

2. Thunder Bay and District Humane Society www.tbdhs.ca

3. BC SPCA www.spca.bc.ca

4. H.E.A.R.T Dog Rescue www.heartdogrescue.com

The Real
Aussie and Otis

"LOOK FOR AUSSIE AND OTIS IN

"WINTER STORM"!"

Printed in Canada